"*Defenestration Day* feels like a partially macabre yet deeply personal account of a trip through purpose, pain and abject relationships. C. bangs around society, charming and offending and hiding in dark places but making noise to render the shadows he tucks away in useless. All the characters read like reflections or memories of people we've all met. Every conversation, no matter if the characters are ensconced in a bedroom or drinking apprehensively at a gallery, feels like script in a film. The book has many cinematic qualities, even in its avant-garde, time jumping form, it still maintains its visceral quality due to the rich minutiae of its cast. It was enjoyable sitting behind the driver seat of C., even though the narrative was the driver, I still felt a bizarre level of control, like the words, thoughts, feelings and decisions of C. were still somehow mine, which is haunting."

— Adam Homer Lawson, author of *Animals on Buses*

"A restless, cautionary tale on the labor of consciousness and the perils of overthinking one's experience. Hertzberg anxiously shows how a writer, once in love with language, becomes tangled in its intricacies and broken by the ways it falls short."

– Sarah Jane Quillin, *fields magazine*

DEFENESTRATION DAY

Andrew Hertzberg

Parafine Press
Cleveland, OH

First Parafine Press Edition 2019
ISBN: 978-1-950843-05-3

Parafine Press
3143 West 33rd Street, Cleveland, Ohio 44109

www.parafinepress.com

Book and cover design by David Wilson

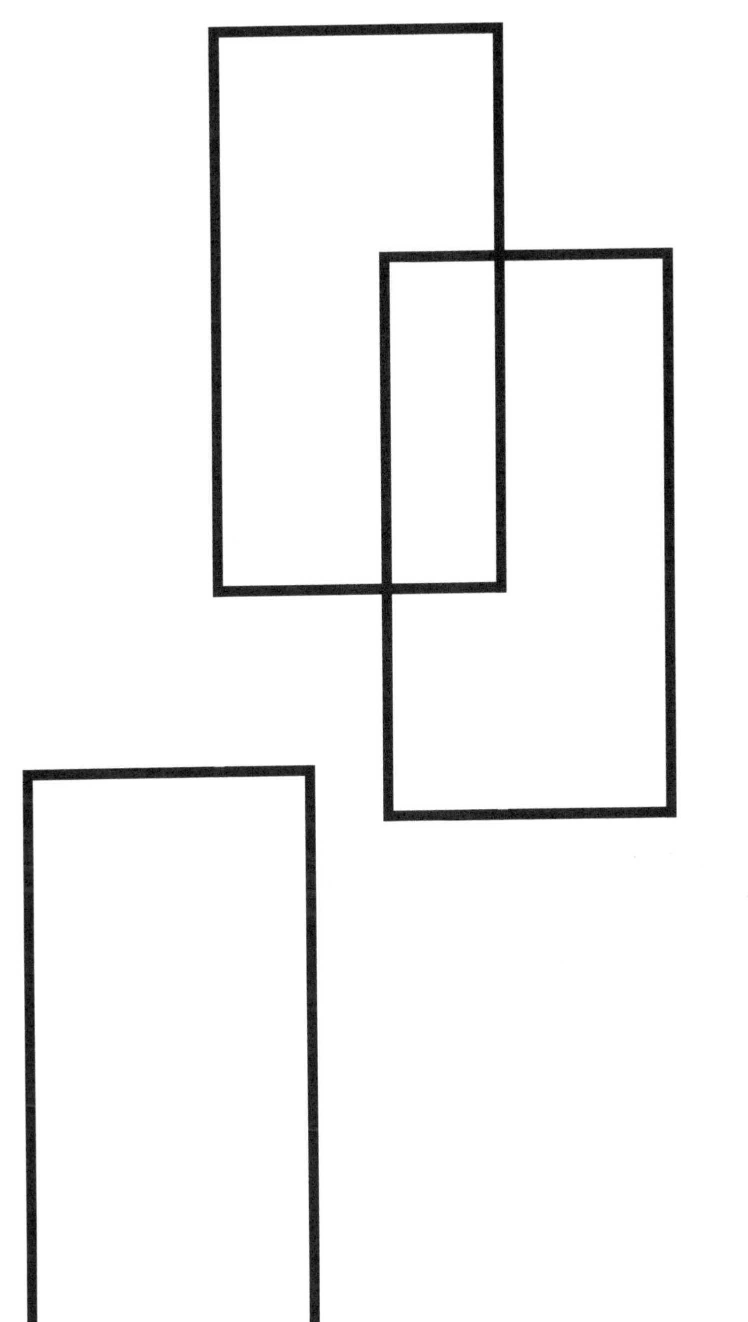

The 20th Defenestration Day

Like everyone else, I used to throw my words out the window. The words that I no longer needed. But I don't celebrate the holiday anymore. I can't.

I remember the first Defenestration Day. Sitting in my windowsill, legs inside with my torso and head sticking out. I remember looking over the wide avenue four stories below. Sleeping cars parked in parallel. Silent streets. No bodies to be found, no people, no stray cats, no swooping birds, not a rat scurrying by. I remember looking at the four-story building across the street, standing on a foundation of graffiti, those spray-painted slogans a defenestration in their own way. Before Defenestration Day I often passed time staring into the hollow windows that lined either side of the curved building. Inside was a labyrinth of peeling wallpaper, abandoned furniture, faulty staircases, and the corpses of so many dreams cut short by the cancers of reality. But on that first Defenestration Day, there was a chance for dreams to become realized. To become fulfilled.

I admit I was nervous that first time. We all were shy, not sure exactly how to celebrate properly. We quickly learned that there was no proper way to celebrate, that it was up to each individual to decide what to do. We were presented with opportunity, with choice. The actions on this day revealed our characters to our friends, our family, our neighbors, ourselves.

Men, women, children, everyone gathered at the windows, the smiles on their faces not enough to express the joy they felt inside, not enough to express their curiosity of this new communal endeavor. This coming together. This new and courageous act of freedom.

As the sun began to rise, howls of release burst onto the city streets, a cathartic muddle of pain, loss, regret, anger, frustration, misery, torment, any and all afflictions spiritual, mental, or physical. Everyone was given a voice after feeling so voiceless. If you weren't too busy screaming out the window yourself, you could potentially parse out a pebble of wisdom here and there.

In the years since, I've developed a keen ear for specific prayers. But there is still a mystery to this holiday. Yes, while I may be able to reduce this roaring throng into its individual components, I am still rarely privy to the enigmatic nature of why people shout what they do.

The origins of the holiday itself are mysterious. Parallels have been drawn to other cultures. For instance, the sons and daughters of the reindeer-herders of the North, who in the months of year when the moon glimmers all day long, feel the need to scream out to their faraway neighbors in a form of call-and-response to signify that their isolation is only temporary. Likewise, Defenestration Day has been considered the verbal equivalent to the sky lantern celebrations in the East, where revelers cast their hopes and dreams up toward the heavens. And maybe it was inspired by burning bowl ceremonies, where people write down on paper what is holding them back in life and burn it in symbolic purification. Maybe screaming out a window is a way to leave behind suffering, regret, pain, sorrow.

When the holiday began, many thought it could be used to relieve stress, to say the things out loud they would normally be reprimanded for. The true feelings for one's boss, a plea for divorce, anti-government protestations, sexual taboos, any questionable or contrarian preferences to popular opinion. But this is what actually happened: given the opportunity to physically and viscerally release one's innermost being, that undefinable *something* that exists within the framework of our bodies, humans will, every time, choose to expel what holiday-scholars declare as "what is immanent within every single person."

(Note: While I do not celebrate the holiday any longer, I am an avid student of the lore surrounding it.)

I have some issues with this theory. The primary issue is that of translation: how to translate immanency into language, language that is not only thought, but also said and then, with equal difficulty, discarded. Is self-sabotage really that integral to the human experience? Anecdotal evidence says this is true. I saw it. I remember seeing it. Or at least I think I remember. Because wouldn't you, if given the chance to scream yourself as part of a crowd, wouldn't you want to express something more than illusory discomforts?

The history of the first Defenestration Day has only become more complicated with time. Stories are told, truths blur, embellishments become reality. Those that claim they were there, probably weren't. The holiday has no religion or political stance or nationality. It emerged spontaneously and spread rapidly. It is most likely the only lingual holiday celebrated in the history of the world, although even that description feels false.

I took notes that first year. It was a series of riddles that I doubt I will ever solve. I scrawled pages trying to understand, to try to find some connections or some clues, but year after year turned up nothing. Here is just a sample from that first year:

I am naked, frozen solid in ice with a crown on my head!

If I don't lay here motionless, I'll be pierced and prodded endlessly...

This cavern is bright and its ceilings never ending!

I am swimming in a vast sea of yellow, cyan, orange, and blood red...

A thousand peacock feathers breathe from the snake's scales inside me!

An egg can only bloom in desert heat!

How do I unlock my head from a tomb made of keys?

These symbols have no definition!

...and so on. The whole day and into evening.

I remember, that first year, after an hour of my own screaming, my own defenestrating, I took a break to enjoy a warm breeze that whistled through the palm trees below. Preparing myself for another round of bellows, I locked eyes with a child in that derelict building across the street. There was a liveliness to her that struck me as being contradictory to the vacuous window in which she sat. She looked at me—patiently, congenially—and I was terrified.

I did not understand why then, but today I know. Although I was always deliberate in the words I personally chose to defenestrate, the utterances of others always boomeranged back to me and I could not get rid of them. In a way, what *they* chose to discard had become a part of *me*. After two decades of celebrating Defenestration Day, I know that my words that day—the ones I expelled, the ones that I could no longer bear—affected her in the same way I have been affected by the words that others threw away. I sent that young girl into a life of complexity, of turmoil, of inner struggles she should never had known had she not been sitting in the windowsill that day. I cannot say I know about her struggles for sure. But it's a feeling. That I did something wrong, even if it was just what everyone else was doing that day.

So many others continue to celebrate every year, even if I cannot anymore, knowing what I know now. Year after year, people return and are thrilled and smile and laugh and cry and convert all of their joy into amorous copulation (though only the truly irredeemable make love on the windowsill on this holiday). The cacophony grows. More people join. The cycle continues. Because only in a society where everyone already talks over one another would we decide to create a holiday devoted to doing just that.

That holiday is today.

The 1st Defenestration Day

When I stopped screaming, the girl had left the windowsill. I felt relieved. Not relieved as in free of anxiety. Relieved of weight. Something had changed. Something changed in me and at first I could not say what that feeling was. There was an emptiness within me I had never felt before, but the chasm of where certainty used to be—where that thing called an identity used to be—was no longer there.

In the past, I used wine to fill that void. Plenty of people were probably drinking wine to celebrate the day, but to me this was supposed to be a day of rebirth. That this emptiness was a way to take everything I thought I knew about my life, the world around me, what existence itself was, to take all of this and redefine it in the image to which I had always sought. This holiday was the baptism I never had.

I took a step back from the windowsill and turned around. I looked around my apartment, to the tattered couch, the taxidermied tortoise, the bar-cart full of ample opportunity for distraction, the framed landscape photography above the bar, the barren-white walls that made up the rest of my studio, the guitar with perpetually broken strings, the hotplate, the small refrigerator, uncontaminated by any food inside. My eyes kept moving along the scratched-up hardwood floor until I spied my pair of scuffed black gym shoes. I put on those shoes and a light coat, then I opened the door, crossed through the threshold, and hurried down the four flights of stairs to the exit.

I had no plan. I looked down 6th Avenue. I looked down Howard. My mind felt clear of thought. Not in a nirvanic sense. I was sterile of thought. Words entered my mind but I failed to wrangle any meaning out of them. Had my actions on this day neutered some part of me? Had it cut myself off from language?

Would I be able to get it back?

Deciding that either street was as good as any other, I walked down Howard. Howard is a busy street, plenty of restaurants, cafes, bars. I would skip the bars, but I needed to eat something. A cafe would be good, a light snack, some water, some coffee. That's all I needed. I'd been screaming all day, and I just needed to eat. I also hadn't expected my throat would be this sore. I needed water.

Of course, nothing was open. (The holiday.) So I kept walking. Somewhere had to be open. I continued along Howard, having passed 9th and 10th Avenues with still nowhere to be found. It was after 11th Avenue that I heard a sound—not a scream, but something melodious. I looked up at the brick building I was standing outside of. I couldn't see anybody, but their words were most decidedly being defenestrated. I listened closer.

Camouflage paint would scare any linguist away.

If gold rusts, what then can iron do?

A token of gratitude makes people shiver

Tout est pour le mieux dans le meilleur des mondes possibles.

I took a notepad out from a jacket pocket and tried to write down what was being said. In those days, I was a writer. Well, at times at least. I did more of other things than I did of writing, but when there was opportunity I tried to sell my stories to anyone who paid. Copying the words from defenestrators, however, was not an original thought on that first holiday. Nothing I wrote down was ever published. But it seemed important to document, if even just for myself. There had to be a connection to what people were screaming out their windows. I refused to believe that it was all meaningless and random and vulgar. So I wrote down everything I heard. I still have every scrap of paper from every Defenestration Day, even after I stopped celebrating it myself.

Suddenly I began to feel dizzy. I was feeling claustrophobic despite being outdoors. Maybe it was the buildings. I was too close to all these buildings. I happened to be on a block where the first floor of every building was grey or tan cinderblock. Never a blood-red or charming cerulean. Not a storefront in sight. The entire block wore a uniform that said "If you ain't from around here, get to going back where you came from."

It was late afternoon at this point and my throat was still a bit sore. I still hadn't found any food, so I headed toward a park where food vendors routinely set up carts. As I walked the few blocks to the park, I noticed some streets were quieter than others, though none were roaring noise and insults the way they would a few years later.

Palm trees swayed along the ever-widening boulevard that eventually led me into the park. I could see the vertical column monument at the center of the park, christened La Fete du Temps by those who created it, supposedly translated from the language of the city's founders. It was sculpted by a distant relative of a local politician to commemorate a particularly celebratory-worth length of time the city had been around for. That length of time, ironically, has since been lost to history. Local residents later decided it was a monument to time itself.

On a normal day, friends and family and lovers would rendezvous at La Fete, as the locals called it, for coffee, for alcohol, for games, for kites, for naps, for secret kisses, missed connections, and torrential heartbreak. This was not a normal day, though. The park was empty of human life. Forgotten by an entire species, just for one day, a species that did everything in their power to maintain this structure, the cleanliness of the environs, the dust off the monument (as monuments to time can truly gather no dust). As else forgotten was any employee or vendor that could have cured my thirst, my hunger, my soreness, my sourness. So I kept walking.

I hadn't spoken to another soul all day it seemed. I screamed and there was that girl across the street, but I wasn't so much speaking to her as I was only communicating with myself. I heard the voices of so many other defenestrators, but that was not any sort of connection.

Closer to home, the defenestrations continued. My nutrient-deprived mind began to wander. I should have been better prepared. How did I not have food at home? What was I doing all week knowing that this holiday was coming? No one really knew what to expect from this day, though. What little media there was in those days (not as bad of a drought as it is now) didn't seem too curious about the event. Nobody could have predicted how significant this holiday would eventually become. Call it the curse of cultural myopia.

I knew I needed to find food but all I could hear around me were voices. I began to hear a familiar voice. No, not a familiar voice but familiar words. I looked to the red-brick building the sounds were coming from. The door was unlocked, and my curiosity dominated my fears of injury or really any form of better judgment. I wasn't one to trespass especially onto a private residence, of which the owner could be in the possession of any number of weapons. Life was safer back then compared to today, but it still wasn't smart to take any chances.

I walked into the dusty apartment building and noticed at the end of a long, dimly lit concrete hallway a wooden stairway, uncarpeted leading up four flights. I couldn't tell where the familiar words were coming from when I was outside. I walked down the hall and got to the stairway, the words barely audible at this point.

There I was, standing in this building I had never been in before, not having eaten all day, confused and curious, tired and groggy, trespassing and not at all suspicious that any harm could be coming my way. Any other day I would have turned around, stuck with my mission of finding just one open restaurant or grocer in this city and returned to my apartment to watch the sun set into itself and resolutely, quietly end another day.

But that day I started up the stairs.

I leaned in close to every door that exited on to the stairway. I listened for a minute, to confirm that I couldn't hear anything. I continued up the stairs, the hall still silent, still barely lit, until the next landing. I leaned into the first door and heard nothing. Kissing my ear to the second door I could then hear some rumblings. Some mumblings. Some somethings. I heard words that I knew, words I remembered, in an order that made sense to me at a previous point in my life. I didn't know what to do. I couldn't knock. Should I have knocked?

I twisted the door knob and the concrete slab began to move. I pushed in slowly, holding my breath. The door was slightly ajar and I could better make out what was being said. I slowly exhaled, slowly took out my notepad, slowly took out a pen, and rapidly began to write.

It was the self, the purpose and essence of which I sought to learn.

It was the self, I wanted to free myself from, which I sought to overcome.

But I was not able to overcome it, could only deceive it, could only flee from it, only hide from it.

What was all this that sounded so familiar? And why did these words seem particularly significant to everything I was feeling and experiencing at this point? I still do not know who said these words and why they resonated so resolutely with me.

Truly, no thing in this world has kept my thoughts thus busy, as this my very own self,

this mystery of me being alive, of me being one and being separated and isolated from all others, of me being…

I was still scrawling furiously in my notepad when the voice stopped mid-sentence.

"Who's there?" they called out.

I didn't move. I heard a chair scrape.

"You better pray to fucking God that you're not standing outside my fucking door right now." The chair scraped again and a glass shattered on the ground. A toddler started screaming and the voice continued swearing and threatening, and I knew I didn't want to stick around to find out whose body that voice was connected to. I turned and rushed down the stairs. I wanted to put obstacles in the way but there was nothing but dust. Despite my weakened condition, I ran and ran and jumped down the stairs two at a time until I reached the ground floor. I pushed open the door to get outside and that's when I ran into her.

Joy.

We helped each other up off the ground.

Her first words to me should have been a sign. "Are you okay?" she asked.

My first words to her should have been equally a sign.

"I'm so sorry," I said hoarsely.

"Was that you screaming those things up there?" She motioned with her head to the window of the apartment I had just ran away from.

"Oh, me, no," I managed to cough out. "I live a few blocks away. I already did my screaming this morning. Wanted to be one of the first, you know."

I grimaced. I scraped my elbow on the sidewalk after falling down but tried not to let it look like it bothered me.

I don't believe in love at first sight, because I don't believe in love at all. I believe in electricity and magnetism and electrodes wanting to explode. I believe in biological actions and chemical reactions. I believe Joy is the most beautiful woman I have ever seen in my life.

I took too much time thinking about this and staring at her awkwardly and tried to regain my composure. "What about you? Did you celebrate today?"

She laughed. I made her laugh. I'd known her less than a minute and I made her laugh. She looked at me. Lightning bolts. Electrons. Volcanoes.

"Well, in the sense that we all have our own ways of celebrating the day, then yes, I suppose I did."

"I'm happy to hear that," I replied, with a goofy smile erupting on my face. "Sorry, I feel kind of dizzy. I guess I've been celebrating so much today, I've forgotten to eat."

"You're hungry?" she asked.

"I am fucking starving," I said more crassly than I intended. She didn't seem to mind. More electrons.

"I know a place that's open nearby. Do you want to join me?"

"I would love to if you can put up with me ignoring you until I eat my weight in food. I must warn you; it's not going to be pretty."

"It can't be worse than your first impression, running out of a building like a madman like that."

"Fair enough. Don't say I didn't warn you."

She took me around the corner, farther from my apartment but I couldn't be bothered to care where I was. It was getting dark but I'd be able to find my way home. We went to a take-out place, the food originating from a faraway land, or so I've been told. I've never actually looked up where this land is. We got our food and sat at a plastic table in plastic chairs outside. The streetlights awoke as the sun's light started to fall asleep.

We enjoyed our meal in silent glances, stifled giggles from her and some satisfied head bobbing from me.

"So what were you screaming about this morning?" she asked me. "What did you feel was so important that you just had to let it out?"

"Well, I can't say it now, of course. But I guess I can give you the gist of it."

She leaned in. Her hair fell in front of her face. I wanted to brush it back.

"I wanted to rid myself of everything I want and everything I don't want. I know we don't always know what we want and we don't know what we don't want. We take these big massive, unexplainable, inexplicable concepts and give them names: desires and fears. But those are both the same in the end. What we put into words can't really describe what we feel. Ultimately, all of language came from one word, right? Well, I think we can get it back to one word. But we don't know what that word is yet."

"For someone railing against words, you sure are using a lot," she replied to my rant.

"I suppose so." I clawed through my memory trying to think of interesting anecdotes, something witty, something strange, something captivating. "I met this old man once. I didn't really meet him. We were on the same bus and he started talking to me. You know, like, talking *at* me. He said he never forgets anything. That his mind is just constantly buzzing with all the knowledge he's accumulated over his sixty-something, seventy-something, whatever odd years it was. He said when he wants to forget something, he writes it down and throws it away. That's stuck with me. I guess I've always sort of felt that way about words, you know? We have so many at our disposal, as a people, as a culture, and there's just still so many opportunities for miscommunication. We keep making the same mistakes every time. Talking is the easiest and the hardest thing to do."

"You make it sound like you're trying to climb the Tower of Babel. Except it's not climbing. It's digging. A Trench of Babel? A Well of Babel?"

I looked her straight in the eye and said as seriously as I could: "A Cave of Babel."

She too looked me seriously in the eye. "A Lair of Babel."

"A Tunnel of Babel," I said.

"A Den of Babel," she said.

"A Rut of Babel."

"A Depression of Babel."

I paused. "A...Grotto of Babel?" At this we both ended up laughing and I will never be able to say why. But we couldn't stop. I couldn't speak. I could barely breathe. We kept laughing. I began that first Defenestration Day trying to both get rid of something inside me and to find something larger outside myself.

In Joy, I found both.

The Night Before the 20th Defenestration Day

"Please don't make me go."

"You promised."

"I know, but I can't," I say into the phone.

"Why not?"

I hate lying to my sister. "Because I don't want to."

"Asshole," Sophia says.

"I mean, I don't want to…you didn't let me finish. I don't want to, you know, go all the way over to the other side of town. I hate that part of town. Bad memories. Plus it takes like two buses to get there. And I can't show up empty handed, so I have to bring a bottle of wine."

"My God you're such a brat. I'll pay for a car for you and I'll reimburse you for the wine, OK? It's her biggest gallery opening and we won't even be there for the main event. She's kind enough to let us go before the opening, get a sneak peak. Maybe you can write something"—I roll my eyes—"and then we'll be on our way. We can grab dinner or something. When was the last time we did that together, huh?"

"Dinner does sound nice," I say. I pause. "I want to get drunk tonight."

"Goddamnit," Sophia whispers into the phone.

"You know how I feel about tomorrow. I need to find a way I can just sleep the whole day away."

"Please don't get drunk tonight. Regardless of what you think of Susan, she's my best friend and I don't want to do anything to embarrass her like bring along my idiot brother who thinks he needs that stuff just to be around people."

"To be around her at least."

"God, you're disgusting. You sleep with my friend, hurl insults at her, and can't even support her at her opening. I thought you were an adult."

"I wish you could see the smile on my face when you say that. You're such a sweetie, Soph," I sing to her. "Sweet-sweet-sweet Soph-ia."

"Listen, I know tomorrow is gonna be rough for you. I know it is. Just come. It will take your mind off things. You can drink. *Not too much.* I'll monitor you. But I want to see you. It's been awhile. Mom and Dad will be happy to know we're hanging out."

"You're paying for a car?"

"Yes."

"And you'll pay me back for the wine?"

"Yes, fine, if it helps."

"I was thinking we'll need two bottles anyway. Tell the car to get here in twenty."

I hang up before she has the chance to protest. Maybe I really am an idiot. Maybe I've just forgotten how to use my words. No matter. As much as I can't stand Susan, her art isn't all bad. She paints. I love paintings and fall too quickly for painters.

Maybe I should try to be nice to her tonight.

I'm gonna get dressed up just in case I get too fucked up and at least I can still look good. And maybe I will write something. Maybe I'll pitch out to a bunch of places. It hasn't been that long since I've written. Ten years? That's not really that long of a time is it?

I get dressed.

The car is waiting outside exactly when I told Sophia to have it waiting for me. She must really want to see me for some reason. That feels good. It's rare for people to want to see me these days.

I get into the seat in the back of the car and shut the door, initiating movement. No music is playing in the car. I think of requesting a song I know the hard drive can find in its database, but I choose to enjoy the silence. I stare out the window, the city almost on fire from the sun refracting off the clouds. If it were to ever rain in this city I swear it would only rain poison. Knowing my fellow citizens, we'd drink it and ask for a second helping.

The car moves at the speed cars do these days, standard safety regulations dictating every such twist of an axel, the Fahrenheit degree of the rubber, every kiss of acceleration, the decibel level of the sensual purr of increasing revolutions per minute, every bit of detail to the point where they've regulated the level of melancholy one can feel when the car begins to slow down, that the journey is over, that a destination has been achieved, and one must now accept the responsibility of exiting the vehicle and return to having control over their own destiny and future destinations.

As it is, the car reaches my destination. Sophia, clever girl. She didn't program the car to stop at a liquor store. I can't tell if it's her general clumsiness or purposeful vindictiveness or some brilliant combination of both. She should know I know where to go in any neighborhood anyway, and especially the neighborhood with the art galleries and especially the subdivision with all of the trendy galleries that Susan has somehow managed to maneuver her way into getting a show.

I step out of the car and walk two blocks up to the store I used to frequent more often, when I used to frequent this area. When I used to frequent Susan's.

I buy three bottles of wine, partially to teach Sophia a lesson, partially because I am sticking with my plan. I leave the liquor store and return to where the car dropped me off to find Sophia standing there.

"Where are you coming from? I told the car to come here ten minutes ago." Then she notices the bag.

"Sophia, it's an art opening. I'm not going to go to an art opening and not have a few drinks. Don't be ridiculous."

"Three bottles?" she exclaims.

"Well, yeah, one for me, one for Susan, and one for... me," I say, sprouting a coy smile on my lips and holding the bag close to my chest like a tiny dog.

"Ugh, whatever. It's still good to see you." She leans in for a hug and I awkwardly throw my arm holding the three bottles of wine around her back.

"It's good to see you, too," I say. "It's probably a good thing for me to get out of the house for a little bit anyway."

"I didn't mean to pressure you. I know this time of year is rough. It's rough for everyone though you know? Just don't… don't make things about you tonight, OK?"

"I would never dream of it," I say and give my head a bob to flip my non-existent hair out of my face.

"Whatever, let's go in."

The 2nd Defenestration Day

The sound of her footsteps receded down the hallway as she entered the bathroom and flicked on the light. I remained sitting at the windowsill in the bedroom. Listening.

It was evening. The screams were sparse at this point. It was easy to decipher what people defenestrated.

Green explodes into red with the right tint

Anything could be true, depending on the context

before during after before during after

Birds chirped, squabbled, yelped, seemingly unphased from what was clearly a day unlike most others.

Rip this heart out of a carpeted chest and start again

Behind the leaves and through the lens is a limerence sky

Fools believe the body to be made of anything but yarn

I took a sip of peppermint tea. I wrote down everything I heard. I was convinced there was a meaning to all of this. I had to understand. It was beyond fascination at this point; it was an obsession. The distance between last year and this one grew exponentially the more I thought about it. I questioned myself more and, simultaneously, grew surer of myself. I had mentioned that emptiness, that what I thought would be freeing was anything but. But. But life's changes don't always have to be negative. They don't always require a weight. They don't always require regret or dust and dirt or noise or deep breaths held before experiencing the unknown. I learned that. I was trying to learn that. There I sat, at the window in the bedroom of Joy's apartment, wondering the same thing so many other people like me around the world wonder: How did I get to be so lucky?

I heard the click of the light turning off as Joy left the bathroom, and the screaming seemed to cease the moment she came into the room.

"Your place is so much nicer than mine," I said.

"You know I don't care about that," she said and stood next to me at the windowsill, her fingers gliding through my hair. "Do you still hear anything?"

"Not really, no," I told her as she lifted my chin to meet my eyes. "Amazing to think it's been a year since we met."

"C.!" Joy exclaimed and took a step back, releasing my chin. "I can't believe I didn't realize." She walked to the doorway and crouched in the frame. I couldn't help but laugh a little bit.

"Joy, come on, it's OK. It wasn't like we knew then we would start being, you know, *this*," I said and latticed my fingers through hers. "I mean, I literally ran into you all flustered from the screaming, and then that embarrassing dinner. I was embarrassed at least. I was so distracted by your eyebrows. Could you tell?"

She laughed. "My eyebrows? You've never complimented my eyebrows."

"Well, consider this my official declaration of my endless devotion to your eyebrows."

Joy gave me a confused look. She stood up, walked over to me and put her arms around my neck. "I just had an idea. Let's go back to that restaurant. As an anniversary-ish celebration. Those noodles were so good."

"That's a great idea. Except that that place closed."

"Damn, really?"

"Yeah, and besides, I have other plans for us tonight. It was supposed to be a surprise for you. But since you figured out what the party was *really* for, I guess you'll just have to fake it. I know you can be good at that, Ms. Actress."

She released my neck and gasped in mock offense. "Well, make me not fake it first," she said coyly. "Then we can go to that party."

"So direct," I teased and walked closer to her. "This is a new you."

"I'm always a new me to you. You still don't even call me by my real name."

"Does that bother you?" I asked.

"Not really," she said and pulled a little away from me. "Besides, what's in a name? Say it once and then it's gone forever, right? It's not yours anymore, as you say. I know if you say my name, you'll lose me. And I like how you talk about that writer from the South and whatever she said about joy without laughter and how long life is and about needing a degree of blindness in order to see and where music goes when it isn't playing." Joy paused. "How can I remember all of these ideas and can't remember the writer's name?"

"And now I really can't tell you," I teased.

"Well then I'll keep acting," she responded. The smile then left her face. "I didn't really know what to expect from you when we met. You were so… different." She paused. "But I think I understand what's going on inside your head now. I feel like I know where I am in this world when I'm with you."

I took Joy in my arms and looked her in the eye.

"You're looking at my eyebrows again, aren't you?" she asked.

"They're just so damn mesmerizing. Like the whole world depends on their perfect balance."

"I'm as much of an Atlas as you are a physicist. But thank you." She released me. "So what's the deal with this party that

I have to pretend I know nothing about? I assume your sister will be there?"

"Yeah, well, a friend of my sister's offered to host it. She's an artist, so I was gonna pretend we were walking into this super-secret art gallery that was in someone's apartment."

"How clever."

I smiled. "You know me."

"I wonder about that sometimes."

"Me too," I said and kissed her lightly on the forehead. "Come on, let's go."

The Night Before the 20th Defenestration Day

Sophia holds the door open for me. Quiet electronic music is coming from somewhere. The room smells like paint. Not like painter's paint, but wall paint. Don't tell me she used wall paint for her art again. She did, didn't she? It's hard to tell. I see about ten paintings hung up around the room. Besides the floor to ceiling glass on the exterior wall, nothing about the interior design is noteworthy. There are three white plastic chairs in one corner. A waist-high counter top that's built into the room is being used as a makeshift bar. I decide to hold on to my bottles of wine.

Susan is at the far end of the room, facing away from us as we enter. She is looking at her painting in that pose she does, her left arm akimbo and her right index finger pushing into her nose. To think I used to find that pose sexy. To her right with his arm around her is Flynn. Two other women I don't recognize are standing at another painting. I assume they are associated with the gallery.

Sophia and I walk up to the artist and her partner.

"Susan," Sophia says.

"Sophia!" Susan exclaims. The two of them hug. Flynn and I nod and shake hands silently.

"Thank you so much for coming!" says Susan. "And you even managed to get your brother to come. That really means a lot to me, thank you both for being here. My first opening—I can't believe it! I've already had two glasses of wine I'm so nervous."

I took this as good of a cue as any. "Hey, it's never too early for me either."

"Sprung for the screw-tops, huh?" says Flynn.

"Flynn's just joking, aren't you honey?" says Susan. "There's plastic cups at the bar. Mind pouring me one?"

Flynn looks at her.

"Oh what, come on, it's *my* opening! I'm allowed. Plus I won't be able to drink for a long time after this anyway."

"Wait, what?" asks Sophia.

"I think I'm gonna go get those cups," I say and turn away from the news. I don't need to hear about pregnancies. What a life to bring another life into. What a world to bring another world into.

I fill up four plastic cups, effectively killing the first bottle of wine. "Congratulations sound like they're in order," I say returning to the group.

"Well, I'm not pregnant yet. But we are trying. I know we're not married, but things just feel so right right now, you know?"

"I literally have no idea what you're talking about," I respond, knocking back half my cup.

My sister looks at me aggressively.

"But!" I attempt to regain a convivial repose. "That doesn't mean I can't be happy for your happiness. To the future young tiny sticky version of Susan and Flynn's DNA."

"Close enough," Susan says, and we all clink plastic.

"Quite the interesting timing of this opening, huh?" my sister says.

"Yeah, well, I didn't want to put it off any longer and I had most of the pieces already finished," says Susan. "It was just a matter of being a locked-up madwoman for a few days to get everything just right. Some of them still don't feel finished. But I'm not thinking about it. I'm not thinking about it."

"Say Susan, have you ever thrown a painting out the window?" I ask.

"Why would I do something like that?" she asks incredulously.

"I don't know, I mean, isn't what's on the canvas supposed to represent your innermost self? Isn't that what we're supposed to throw away?"

I see Sophia and Flynn look at each other.

"Well, I guess I look at it like throwing paint on the canvas *is* my way of throwing myself on it," Susan responds. "Or of throwing myself away as you seem so fond of saying."

"That is one theory I suppose," I reply. "But once it leaves you, is it still you? What I mean is this: you take your hand, you grab the wooden handle of the brush, right? At the end of the brush are bristles. You dip them into paint—store-bought, of course, it's all store-bought. But into this paint, you dip these bristles, which are connected to the wood handle, which is connected to your hand. But then! But then you press the brush to the canvas, diligently and purposefully applying this paint that has become an extension of yourself onto the canvas, or perhaps you let it drip onto it from above. And then? And then what? What's the connection?"

"So, what about you and your stories?" Susan asks. "Are your stories a part of you once your store-bought pen lifts from the store-bought paper? Or what about when you type out words onto a screen? If you want to talk about distance, what is more distancing than typing things onto a screen?"

"I'm not here to talk about my words, Susan. We're here for your paintings," I laugh and gesture around.

"Oh, I think I see now," Susan says. "Are you asking me about this for your article? Trying to get some juicy gossip or something?"

"What do you mean?" I ask, legitimately confused.

"Sophia told me you were going to write an article on the exhibit," Susan confesses.

"No, I didn't mean, I think I suggested, he *could* write an article on the exhibit," Sophia stammers. "Look, I mean, no pressure, but you've been looking to get back into writing again..."

"Sis, it's OK. No, I'm not doing too much writing these days. That's all."

Now it's Susan who looks confused. "I thought you were

a journalist?"

"A journalist!" I laugh.

"And why that tone?"

"Journalists have to be objective," I say. "I've read too much. Hell, I've lived too much. My world is too wide. I've learned what it takes to be present. Aware and present. Journalists are aware but they aren't present. They can pretend to be, but they aren't. They have to be aware and disappear at the same time."

Now it's Susan who laughs. "Oh, come on. Then why do you always say things with this air of objectivity?"

"I do not," I defend, but Susan laughs again.

"The fact that you're not even aware of that does prove how subjective you are. But you also try to be objective. Stating opinions as facts all the time."

"Just because I am confident in my opinions doesn't mean I don't believe there isn't room for others. I don't believe in equality when it comes to everyone having the same exact thoughts. I believe in inequality of thought, I guess you could say, if only to keep the world an exciting place."

"So if everyone's always shouting over each other, do we become more or less equal? Or more to the point, how do you really feel about my art?"

"Don't answer that question," Sophia jumps in, but I already have my response in the chamber.

"I write when I feel it is necessary. So if I think your art is necessary, I'll write about it."

Susan glares at me, trying not to let her anger show.

"Well. In that case. I'll keep an eye out for your article sometime next week." She hands he plastic cup to Flynn and walks to the other side of the gallery to inspect another painting. Flynn stands for a moment with both cups in his hand, shakes his head at me, and walks over to Susan.

"Damn it, C., what is your problem?" Sophia growls.

"Oh come on, I was only joking. She used to be more fun,

you know."

"You used to be less of a jerk, you know."

"I can't seem to recall," I say and finish off my cup of wine. "Well, I'm all out of pleasantries." I take the last of the wine bottles in my hand. "If you'll excuse me, my date and I have somewhere to be."

"You're not serious."

"I've already managed to offend the artist before the show even opens. Not sure how great of an idea it is for me to try to apologize right now."

"And what are you and your date going to do?"

"I'm going to drink her, and her ruby red lipstick is gonna stick to my teeth."

"I can't believe you sometimes. I can't believe I'm doing this, but I'm coming with you. Let me just say goodbye to Susan."

"We'll be waiting outside for you." I don't even try to look in Susan's direction on my way out. I swear I'm not always this vindictive. I don't even know why I became so just now. Something has happened within me, my ideal of me, my vision of what I am, what defines me, is not replicated in my actions. It's a tired story to everyone who is close or has ever been close to me. Always saying that tomorrow will be better, I will match my ideal self. But that is never the case. I dig down deeper and deeper into who I really am as defined by actions, no matter how opposite of my thoughts they are. I haven't stood on solid ground in years. It's not the earthquakes. It's not the violent outbreaks around the country. Everyone else manages nature and society on a level that I cannot attain. Or will not. Whichever it is, I do not.

I think to myself what would be the things I need to become fulfilled, to plug this hole inside me, to fill this trench, to light this tunnel. The cave inside me is ever-expanding and the deeper I go in an attempt to discover myself, the more lost I become. My fingernails are black from the soil inside me I claw at every day. I only manage to find more dirt. I know soil is necessary for life but what blooms on the surface is never concerned with what makes it grow underneath.

The 3rd Defenestration Day

The Characters

JOY

C.

Man's voice offstage [this role can be played by multiple people or not, performed live or pre-recorded]

Woman's voice offstage [this role can be played by multiple people or not, performed live or pre-recorded]

Setting

A domestic space decorated in the style of the time and place Joy and C. happen to be in, at the age they each happen to be, and the amount of money they both make. One of them makes a large amount more money than the other. There are closed windows on either side of the stage but rain can be seen collecting on them. In the background throughout the entirety of the scene, music that was considered "cool" at the time should be playing. Constant screaming can be heard right before the curtain rises. The two characters Joy and C. have been arguing for some amount of time already, at least minutes, as long as years.

JOY: I don't know why you've never been able to accept me for who I am.

C.: That's just not true.

JOY: It absolutely is. You've always wanted me to be an ideal of something I am not and can't accept that I am who I am because of what I do and say. That's what makes me, me! You live on an imaginary plane sometimes and I try so hard to put up with it because I love you but it's been wearing me down. I don't know how much longer I can be dragged down with you.

C.: Listen to yourself. You're the one trying to tell me

how I think. Two years and you still don't know what is going on in my head.

JOY: Because you refuse to let me in. I mean it when I say I love you, but I have no idea what love means to you.

C.: Love is a series of electric signals following a current through—

JOY [interrupting]: Current through which chemicals are released to manipulate a body into sexual desire to stimulate the forces behind procreation. Yes, I know, you've said it a million times. But you sound like a goddamned book when you say that. I want to know what it is that love means to *you*.

C.: Joy, you haven't been listening.

JOY: Stop talking. Think. Just think about that word. Love. Close your eyes. [C. does] Just think about that word. [calmly] What are you thinking of? Who are you thinking of? Of me? Your mother? Your sister? Art and music and mountains and sunsets? What do you feel? Don't tell me. Just feel.

C. [slowly]: I do see you. I…I feel you. I feel your hand, no, I feel a presence that I believe is you. I…I see my family. I see a lake, a frozen lake. I see mountains on fire. I hear a marimba. It's…it's making me sway. I…I am not in control. All of this is out of my control. Love is letting go. I am accepting the world as it is. Refusing control. I can feel…I can feel the electric signals from my brain telling me to let go. No, this is all an illusion.

JOY: This will never work.

C. [snapping out of his revelry]: This? What is this?

JOY: Everything. All of it. The last two years. I waited too long.

C. [cynically]: Waited too long for what?

JOY: Don't you already know?

C. [incredulously]: And you'd actually do that?

JOY: Have you given me a choice?

C.: Can't you answer a question without another question?

JOY [pissed off]: Do you think I'm blind?

C.: Do I think you're blind?

JOY: I know you're not deaf. Do you think I'm blind?

C.: Why do you ask that?

JOY: I saw you and her at the party.

C.: Me and who?

JOY: The artist or whoever. I saw you rubbing her shoulder.

C.: I can't rub a shoulder?

JOY: Can't you stop asking questions?

C.: So you saw me rubbing a shoulder.

JOY: Yes.

C.: And you never said anything.

JOY: Yeah.

C.: Why not?

JOY: You know why.

C.: Search me.

JOY [a shake of the head, a roll of the eye, something to show how fucking dim C. is being right now]: Because of everything we defenestrated before it happened! [C. sits down on a piece of the modern furniture that's in the room] Our jealousies, our irrational angers, our pasts. We said we weren't going to let those things affect our relationship.

C.: Ha!

[Throughout the rest of the scene, we realize that what Joy says may or may not have been what actually happened but is only C.'s account of the story. Likewise, the things C. says may or may not have actually been what he said but are only to the best of his recollection, or perhaps he's trying to make himself look better with the blessing of hindsight. The narrator also realizes he's still probably saying problematic shit even when trying to cast himself in the best light because he's anxious his flaws are overtaking his own perceptions of what is going on around him. The reality of the situation might have been quite different.]

JOY: Are you laughing right now?

C.: If you defenestrated that then you wouldn't have been jealous of me. And you wouldn't be angry right now. And you'd stop being so irrational.

JOY: C., you were there! You heard me. You can't deny your own experience.

C.: You did something to nullify it. I don't know what. You crossed your fingers? I don't know what it takes to defy a defenestration.

JOY: Because you've never been defiant in your life.

C.: Let's not go there tonight. This is about you. And whatever witchcraft you pulled.

JOY: [laughs] Witchcraft! Now who's being ridiculous?

C.: What did you do? What did you do so that your words you threw away didn't shatter on the ground?

JOY: C., listen to me, please, this day is not what you think it is. We've talked about this and you only ever hear what you want to hear.

C. [angered]: No, you need to listen to me! Because I am doing everything I can in order to be heard and it is still never enough for you.

JOY [scared]: I don't like seeing this part of you. It seems that no matter how much you scream you will always want to scream more. And I don't know how much longer I can handle that. I'm so sick and tired of screaming.

C. [laughs, not maniacally, but ominously]: Don't you get it? That's exactly *why* we need to keep on screaming.

JOY: So do you keep on screaming until you've nothing left?

C.: I don't make up the rules.

JOY: But there's more to life than this.

C. [stands up, walks to the window at stage right]: You're so sure about that?

JOY: C., don't, stay with me, we can talk through this, we don't need to resort to that.

C. [opens window, rain can be heard, the voices from

outside get louder; the stage director can change phrases from MAN'S VOICE OFFSTAGE and WOMAN'S VOICE OFFSTAGE as they see fit]: If nothing else has worked before now, then what have I got to lose?

JOY: You will lose me! Do you care for me so little?

C. [turns away from audience, leans out the window]: Long cross-country train rides with her head resting on my shoulder!

MAN'S VOICE OFFSTAGE: The outpouring of goodwill only leads to tears of the devil!

WOMAN'S VOICE OFFSTAGE: From time immemorial memorials have been on time!

MAN'S VOICE OFFSTAGE: Does our majestic hero exist in plains beyond the mountains?

C.: The first lash of the whip and especially the last!

WOMAN'S VOICE OFFSTAGE: At least that if no more, thought through my eyes.

MAN'S VOICE OFFSTAGE: A wave loudly clashing against a long shoreline is fucking cosmopolitan, having a trained assassin stay overnight, letting heartbreaking lies roll over us like a summer breeze.

C.: Her fingers curled in a C chord on the ukulele!

WOMAN'S VOICE OFFSTAGE: Name and memory solace thee not.

[Joy can be seen growing increasingly angry as C. defenestrates all of their shared experiences out the window]

MAN'S VOICE OFFSTAGE: The flow of quizzes is often one floor above you.

[C. glares at Joy]

JOY: So this is what you want.

[while the director can mostly feel free to change the exact phrasings of these defenestrations, there must be three female voices that are heard before Joy's first defenestration; the defenestrations can either be original or quote public domain works of literature]

WOMAN'S VOICE OFFSTAGE: Humanity like worms struggling blindly toward inevitable annihilation…

[Joy opens the window on stage left]

WOMAN'S VOICE OFFSTAGE: …seductive, never ceasing, whispering, clamoring, murmuring…

[Joy faces away from the audience, sticks her head out the window]

WOMAN'S VOICE OFFSTAGE: The voice of the sea speaks to the soul!

[Deep breath from Joy, everything should go silent at this point, even the music that has been mostly in the background of this scene. While the audience understands this silence only amounts to two seconds, they also need to feel that this is a moment lost to time, both succinct in its action and timeless, that this was the moment that Joy escapes C.]

JOY: A love that blurred the realities of man and woman.

MAN'S VOICE OFFSTAGE: Abstraction jumps both ways.

C.: Her eyes as eternal as the sky but as black as dirt.

WOMAN'S VOICE OFFSTAGE: …but whatever came, she had resolved never again to belong to another than herself.

JOY: This was never meant to be a crime…

MAN'S VOICE OFFSTAGE: Significant understanding lay down on the riverbed.

C.: I'd kill for that smile…

WOMAN'S VOICE OFFSTAGE: …necessarily vague, chaotic, and exceedingly disturbing…

JOY: Orange used to make green turn to yellow

MAN'S VOICE OFFSTAGE: Tomorrow wants the truth!

C.: The mole above her eyebrow like a setting sun over the ocean!

WOMAN'S VOICE OFFSTAGE: listen listen listen listen listen listen listen

JOY: Nothing ever happens at our favorite intersections anymore!

[Voices can still be heard offstage in the background, but they are less clear and Joy and C. should perpetually be going back and forth, essentially shouting over each other for the next few lines]

C.: Full throttle on the gravel!

JOY [for the first time, vindictive]: A Grotto of Babel!

[At this, both Joy and C. pause. They both have a revelation. Just as before, the music stops, and even though this silence only lasts for two seconds in the experience of the audience, there is also an unmistakable timeless quality that is felt when something is said that can't be unsaid.]

C.: Waving a black flag because I surrender!

JOY: A Rut of Babel!

C.: Denim doesn't stop the rust!

JOY: A Tunnel of Babel!

C.: The glare off the pyramids in Cairo!

JOY: A Cave of Babel!

C. [turns away from the window to face Joy]: And what sense does it make that you're with me if I'm not well?

JOY [turns around]: Love isn't perfect, goddamn it! I wanted to work! I was ready to work. I'm just as imperfect as you are, and I thought I found someone who could take me at my faults as I took him at his. This wasn't superficial for me, do you understand? This… [turns to face out the window and screams] wasn't superficial for me!

C. [looks briefly across the stage and then back out the window; the rain stops momentarily and only his voice can be heard]: Joy! Joy! Joy!

[a beat / the rain begins again]

JOY [breathes deep through her nostrils, most likely inaudible to the audience, walks away from the window leaving it open, and runs offstage]

C. [walks around the apartment, in apparent disbelief]: You can't scream your arms around a memory.

[C. begins to cry. He goes to the kitchen and grabs a jar

from the cupboard. He cries into it. He seals the jar, throws it out the window, and the shatter is heard on the ground outside. He knew it was only a holiday for language, but part of him wanted to believe that if he threw away that jar he would never be sad over her again. It didn't work.]

CURTAIN.

The Night Before the 20th Defenestration Day

I'm standing against a wall down the street from the gallery. I take a pull from the wine bottle.

"I can't believe you," Sophia calls after me. "Can you please not? I am not getting arrested with my lunatic brother."

"A lunatic! Hey everyone! Everyone! We've got a lunatic here!" I begin to taunt her.

"Shut up."

"Sophia, you really shouldn't throw words like that around. Consider the origins of the syllables in the word 'lunatic.'"

She catches up to where I'm standing and crosses her arms. But she listens.

"You see 'luna' means 'moon' in Spanish, but before that, 'lun' meant 'darkness concealed' in Latin. However there are various translations and interpretations of what this could mean. Is it darkness that is concealed or darkness itself that does the concealing? More to the point, is that confusion of meaning actually necessary to meaning in itself? We then have the phrase 'tic.' No, Sophia, it has nothing to do with skin-burrowing forest bugs, but rather it has to do with impulse, with things we can't control, verbal or physical. In this case, it sounds like my tic of a lunatic is verbal. Because otherwise would somebody stare at the moon while screaming at the stars!"

I lift my head upwards and scream.

"You are so full of shit," Sophia says.

I smile. "But I did have you going for a minute there, didn't I?"

"You can barely speak English, let alone fucking Latin."

"Hey now, why the cursing? Do you know the origin of the word 'cursing'?"

She doesn't take the bait and only glares at me.

"OK, fine, I'm sorry. OK? I'm sorry. I honestly did not come tonight with the intent of ruining Susan's opening or whatever. It just sorta came out. It was a tic," I say unironically. "Besides, you're the one that made me come out tonight. Remember that?"

"Yeah, because I thought for once you were going to think about someone besides yourself. This meant a lot to Susan, which means it meant a lot to me. You're my brother so I thought you'd realize that instead of making everything about you again. It's not like you can't see this pattern in your life. I mean, why do you think it is that tomorrow is so difficult for you? You're holding on to something that happened 15 years ago."

"13 years ago."

"Whatever. The point is, things change, man. They fucking change, whether you want them to or not and you can either change with them, or get lost along the way and drink yourself to death." She finishes her little rant, takes the bottle from my hand, and drinks.

"It's not just what happened that day. It's what's happened since then. Or what hasn't happened …"

I pause.

"Let's go there."

"Go where?" Sophia asks.

I tilt my head and raise my eyebrows.

"Oh no. You said you could never go there again."

"I've said a lot of things in my life I don't mean. Does that make them any more or less true? Does that make them more or less a part of me?"

"I hate when you get abstract."

"And yet you like Susan's art. Let's go."

"You're sure?"

"I'm sure."

"I swear if you have another meltdown over there…"

"That's just the risk you have to take with a brother like me," I say and playfully punch her in the arm. "Let's walk. It'll be nice." She takes another sip of wine and hands the bottle back to me.

We walk. We walk on sidewalks and up and down stairs. We walk through parks and under expressways. We drink from the bottle of wine and no one seems to care the way people used to care about this sort of thing.

I have this image of the past, that things were never this complicated and never this easy. There are greater freedoms now but there is more tragedy. In one sense, I experience a level of freedom never felt by man since the advent of politics. In another sense, political systems still prevail, and my existing within this system is another form of dependence and reliance. And craving. Could I exist without this system? When I make small rebellions, like drinking from this bottle, it is really me saying: Give me more of you, I need to drink you in, I need to feel your plutocratic soil beneath my feet and eat your sanitized food and breathe in your black air and smell the turgid greed and worship the plasticity of celebrity. Give me your dirt, your molecules that choke, I am addicted to your fame.

Is this how man is supposed to live? And yet, it is how we live, whether it's what the Earth had intended or not. We are here, in this moment. Change is inevitable and the inevitability about change is that its invisible maneuvers obscure the direction it intends to flow. This country is the worst surprise party anyone has ever thrown.

I don't say any of this to Sophia. Birds cry over our heads. We walk in silence save for the sloshing of what little wine remains in the bottle. A quiet breeze is charming; some of the palms whisper secrets to each other. At another point in my life I would consider this sufficiently buzzed, but now I am scanning my brain's navigation systems to determine the closest place to refuel.

"We're almost there aren't we?" Sophia asks, breaking the silence.

"Not too far," I respond. I dismiss the idea of the pit-stop. We walk a few more blocks and the buildings start to give way to openness. The sea reveals itself, the mountains smirk in the distance.

"There," I say and we can now see the former site of La Fete.

Sophia stops walking. "Oh my God," she whispers. "I haven't been here since..."

"I know," I say. We are standing at the top of the hill, overlooking what used to be a monument to time. It is no more. "We don't have to go down there. Here," I sit down. "Let's just sit on the grass. Let's just... just take it all in."

I remember the rows of trees lined like soldiers that led to the monument to time. The air quality, which naturally changed from day to day but retained a sense of comfort, of clarity, of presence: my breath was never not there at La Fete. And the sounds. The call of birds to their peers, children crying for their parents, the blades of helicopters twirling overhead, steel drums and acoustic guitars from street musicians, the heat of young lovers spreading across the park and beyond, back when love was natural and never forced, before love was swiped from the heart of humanity by the claws of consumerism and advertising and digitization. Or do I only imagine this is what La Fete was like? Maybe it was filled with trash. Maybe it was filled with discarded needles and cardboard homes and musk. Maybe it was filled with violence and desperation. Maybe it wasn't filled with hearts under arrest but young people with nowhere else to go led in handcuffs to places that they never would have considered home.

Maybe both of these places were true. Maybe one place can be both in the same.

Maybe I was asleep whenever I was at La Fete. Maybe I

never really understood where it was that I was living. That I purposefully blinded myself to the social ills of my society, by the abrasions left by a government armed with a lash and lead, that anytime I almost woke up to what was happening around me I reset the alarm to fall back into a deep rest, where I could be transported to another world. I must have been asleep.

I must have fallen asleep. Sophia jabs at my ribs with her elbow.

"What, hey, what?" I stammer.

She does not say anything but points. My eyes need a moment to focus and at first I am not sure I am looking at. A blur, a mass, a muddle, a huddle. Limbs, faces, bodies marching in, through, and around the former site of La Fete. The limbs are holding signs that I cannot read from this distance up on the hill. There is movement but there is no sound. No clapping. No chanting. The sound of footsteps barely audible for the cloth over their footwear. My, the effort it takes to not be noticed these days.

I can only assume this march is in protest to the holiday tomorrow. Have they all been hurt as much as I? Is this an expression of pain through community? Do I dare join them? I attempt to stand up but falter, the effects of the wine combined with a brief respite eliminating my sense of equilibrium.

"Where do you think you're going?" Sophia laughs.

"I mean, they! Them! I should be with them," I try to explain.

"A silent protest? You? You think you're capable of that right now?"

I pinch my right index finger and thumb and draw them across my lips like a zipper.

"That's believable," Sophia scoffs.

I unzip. "Look, you're the one that was just getting on my case for living in the past. Now I want to do something about it and you're pushing me to inactivity?"

"C., if you were in a better state of mind maybe, but I'm not taking my eyes off of you after what you did to Susan. I'm still pissed off about that, by the way."

I sit back down and observe the marchers from afar.

Reader, trust me when I say that you have never heard a silence this profound. Whether this was an anti-holiday movement or a preservation of vocal chords until the official festivities tomorrow, I cannot say. Nor do I know how much of a mark this will leave on me after today. If the last decade has been any indication, I know not what travesties await, about what feelings of heartbreak await, of what failures, treasons, delirium await. Nor could I have predicted all the noise. Do molecules ever get tired of all this forced pressure from the people on this planet? The way we force air to move without its consent? How much suffering could be alleviated in the world were we to live in silent protest every day of our lives?

But then, we would seem mad. Communication is integral to the human experiences of the rulers and the privileged classes that purposeful muteness would be taken for madness. One would no doubt be locked away or deported to a land which is not their home. I have seen this and not seen this so many times to ignore this reality. And what else can I do besides scream? All of this screaming and it leads to nothing. Perhaps that is why they march in silence. It is a new way to gain attention. A new way to communicate. A new way to reverse the ravages of time.

The 7th Defenestration Day

We never asked: where do the words go that we defenestrate? There are theories, but we still do not know.

It should be easy to track. It should be easy to track all of the things we throw away, to understand where it goes, who it affects. Who is affected by the words we throw away? By the words we scream so carelessly? By words that we think we know the meaning of but use indiscriminately, whether defenestrated or in conversation? Conversations still exist. Communication still exists. Conversations and communication matter. They matter no matter how much it may seem like no matter to be able to converse, to commune. These were things that used to take effort. Substantial effort, life-draining and -affirming effort. Being able to effortlessly communicate and converse allowed language to be more playful. It was a radical new dynamic to language. But the playfulness blurred the meaning of communications. Everything came to mean nothing. But nothing did not mean everything. There was a mathematical contradiction that refused to resolve itself through language, through communication.

Is that why there is Defenestration Day? Because we needed to subtract the excess of language from society? But through subtraction created division. People were more and more divided and there was no way to anticipate that division. Then perhaps it was a problem with translation. Because if subtraction can equal division, then addition can mean multiplication. Everything created in this world has been exponential. That includes the dirt.

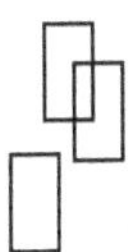

One's experience is primarily rooted in the experience of others. It is why we crave stories. Watching others experience heartbreak or pain or happiness or ecstatic feelings or boredom or hate allows us to discover how we might act in those same situations. How we think we might act in those situations. The truth of the matter is that no matter how many stories we read, how many movies and television shows we watch, how much gossip we hear and eavesdropped telephone conversations on the bus, none of it ever prepares one for how to feel in a situation. There are no rules to life anymore. One is tempted to believe that the only ethical course of action is the feeling of nothingness. Absence is moral. Sometimes. Not all times.

I reflected on these thoughts at a time in my life when absence was a cruel and persistent constant in my life. I've been told my whole life that I focus on the things I do not have, that I focus on the things that are not there. And perhaps I did and still do. Is that why this holiday resonates so well with me? Because I am at least able to know how little everyone else has? They all appear to have these words, so many nouns and adjectives thrown away. What do I get to throw away? Floss. Tissues. Plastic boxes that used to hold plastic food. A ripped sock here and there. But now I get to throw away these words. These phrases. These idioms and ideas and id-infused rants. I get to be a part of something bigger than me. I get to celebrate with humanity, I get to participate with the rest of the world in something.

By the seventh year, the holiday had grown across the world. In my mind, this was a good thing. No borders, no religions. A holiday anyone could celebrate. I was naïve. I should have seen what was coming.

Language is more dangerous than borders, more coveted than religions. It is a perilous venture, perhaps mankind's worst contribution to itself. Wars are started and ended over gods, but man will continue to bully and insult and confuse and mock and unleash every part of his linguistic arsenal, continue to launch cannonballs of deceit, continue to yam and yawn and yarn the twine of words around his enemies necks. Power and stupidity and violence are natural to all animals, but pure villainy can only be found in the one that devised language.

I don't remember the first explosion I heard, and I don't remember the last explosion I heard. There may have only been one explosion. I remember fires. I remember piles of brick that used to make up buildings. I remember thinking my neighborhood looked like a cemetery with all of the tombs above ground. I remember the crying of children, the laughter of those in disbelief. I remember the sky was orange and yellow and red, but I don't remember ever actually looking at the sky itself. I remember the way palm trees on fire reminded me of fireworks at the time. I remember the smells. Not just of excessive smoke, of gasoline, of burning plants, of burning flesh, but also of sulphur, but whether I imagined that smell or actually experienced it, I doubt sometimes. I remembered all of the movies and media about volcanoes I had ever seen but this destruction was not caused by a polluted and petulant planet seeking revenge. This was the work of man when confronted by language he did not agree with. Confronted by language he found distasteful, disgusting, distant, disordered, and disobedient.

Words men disdained. Disdained to the point where they required flames.

Man can only have so much dirt piled on him until he retaliates. Or think that there is this dirt being piled on him. Man is convinced, is conned by himself, more than he is convinced or conned by others. There is more truth in fiction than we want to recognize. What truths were they missing when they attacked our city? What lies did they depend on to construct their identities? What lies supported the beds they slept in and jump-started their mornings? Why did they think that what we were doing existed to be more against them than it existed to be more for us?

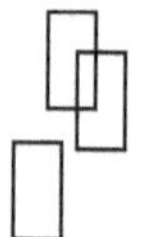

Initial news reports said that the explosion was caused by a suicide bomber. Or multiple bombers. That is the most convenient way for a government to capitalize on the terror already experienced by its citizens. Governments rely on terror for power. Citizen investigators, with no large media outlet to obey, began to decry this reason. Some went as far as to say it was the government itself that was the cause of it. But this was quickly debunked, despite how some people still believe it today.

I couldn't tell you how many people were in the park that surrounded La Fete that day. If there was a man with a cart selling corn and syrup-sweetened sugars. If he was playing music while he did so. I couldn't tell you the types of birds that circled around the sky, the sounds they made, the colors hidden in their wings and hearts. I couldn't tell you how many children there were, that would never grow up. How many families, subtracted, divided, or completely rounded down to zero. How many lovers perished with their lips entangled with another, how envious I was of that at the time. To die like that. To have lived like that.

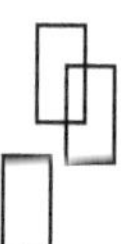

I remember seeing her right before it happened. It'd been years since I'd seen her but I knew it was her. She was sitting on a bench. Reading. Reading a book on a day meant for repose, reflection. I do not know what book it was or what kind of book it even might have been. Is that a detail that matters?

What if I had noticed her five minutes sooner? Would I have walked down to her? See how she's been doing all these years. Wonder why the two of us never caught up, grab a coffee, laugh and pretend we were both fine with the way things ended.

I saw her for one moment. She was gone in the next. She turned into an explosion, into flames, layers of inferno, she became ashes, dust; she was subtracted from the world.

She became what was left in my mind, which wasn't much because I'd been screaming about her to forget her all these years. It's what I was doing earlier that morning. I screamed and I screamed and I screamed. Her name. Our memories.

Camouflage paint is a storyteller without equal.

Significant understanding comes asking for bread.

A late night tells the tale of towers.

I'd given up so much of her that she was already incinerated in my mind. I could remember nothing of her but ashes, but dust.

What I saw that day, the terror all around me, the chaos, the extremity. I couldn't cry. No matter how hard I tried. I felt nothing.

I remember thinking: this won't be the last time this happens. Until we think about what it means to defenestrate, where our words go when we put them out in the world, this will continue to happen. I remember thinking that I was a part of the problem. That I was complicit. I don't know if I felt guilty about this complicity but I just knew the complicity. I didn't know if I would change. How much can one change and how much does it matter when the damage is already done?

After that, I couldn't scream anymore.

The Night Before the 20th Defenestration Day

The last of the marchers disappear into the distance. Sophia and I remain sitting on the grass for a minute without speaking. It was quieter when the protest was here, I think but do not say. Because there was the potential to speak, that they all chose to remain silent, in that way makes everything even quieter.

"Let's go," Sophia says.

"Where are we going?" I ask. "We're out of wine."

"I know. We're going for a walk."

"We've already walked enough. Or do you want to go back to Susan's?"

"No. But I do have a place in mind. We can sneak wine in there if you really want."

We walk through the city. It is starting to get dark out. There is a quiet settling over the city, as it happens around this time of the holiday every year. I follow my sister with an idea of where we may be heading but I do not reveal this. She stops in a liquor store for a bottle of wine; I wait outside. I twiddle my thumbs. I try to think of the origin of why people ever twiddled their thumbs, about the simplicity of such an action and how much meaning can be derived from that action. I think about the ubiquity of mobile devices. About the daily *deus ex machina* such devices provide. About how we twiddle our thumbs in a different pattern along a flat screen, about how we all gladly succumbed to this technology that no one ever asked for. Was that really the evolutionary endgame? To create devices to do everything? To rid ourselves of our Selves? My sister better come out soon.

I stare at the sky. The sky. So many pictures we take of the sky. As if it's possible to forget it was there. So many pictures of the clouds, of the moon, of the stars when they're not shielded by the glow of urban lights.

I stare at the tattoo on my wrist. It is of the letter E. My grandfather was an optometrist. I got the tattoo in honor of him, for all the eye-sight test cards they used to use with E facing in different directions. These were useful for people who couldn't speak English. They were called "illiterate cards" or "dummy cards." A different world back then. I got the tattoo in honor of him but also in honor of my family's immigrant past. My grandfather would have been considered illiterate. He would have been considered a dummy. But he overcame. He defied his otherness. I am doomed to end the lineage of our family without honoring the generations that came before me. I feel guilty about this procreational brick wall. Some days. Not often.

My sister walks out of the liquor store, and I know where she is taking me.

"The cemetery?" I ask. "Really?"

"Yes. Do you have a reason we shouldn't?"

"No, not at all," I respond. "I just, it seems so random. You want to see our grandparents, or what?"

"I don't know, it seems like a place where no one is going to be screaming or protesting or doing anything in there. We can just walk and be and talk and just be you and me. We can try to alleviate some of your anxiety."

"With the wine."

"Well, yeah, with the wine."

I nod my head, grab the bottle from her, and we walk along.

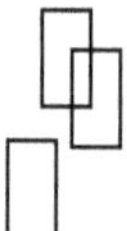

We reach the cemetery and Sophia was absolutely right. Not a living soul in sight. We have the entire place to ourselves. The cemetery is not large, nor particularly well-kept. But it is where the decomposing versions of our family members lay. It is where I will most likely lay someday myself. Although it's not particularly important to me to be buried here, I feel I won't have much say in the matter once my heart decides it's had enough.

The grass around us is brown and dry. It crunches under our feet. In the history of man, no burial ground has ever looked so desolate and forgotten. It is depressing and not just for the way it should be depressing. I twist the cap off the bottle of wine, take a sip, larger than I'd intended, and wipe my stained lips onto my white shirt, leaving behind a boozy kiss. But I am clearly past the point where I care.

The sun is not completely down but light posts guide our path through the cemetery.

"Do you know where he's buried?" I ask Sophia.

"Sort of. I have an idea. Shit, it's been years since I've been here. Does that make us bad grandkids?"

"Well, we never see Mom and Dad, who are still alive, so we're definitely bad kid-kids. Hard to say if not seeing someone who can't see you makes you a bad descendent."

"Fair point. I still feel guilty."

"More so than when we put them in a home?"

"It was for their own good," Sophia snaps. "Were you going to take care of them?"

"No, I mean, obviously, there's no way I could do that," I reply. "It's just, you know, you never can tell if you've done the right thing until time passes, right? I've never felt right or wrong with my relationship with our parents. It just sort of is. It is what it is as they say. It just is."

Sophia squints at me. "Best give me that wine." I concede. I continue to look around the cemetery as we wander and search for our grandparents, buried side by side, somewhere. There are graves that were reburied here when the city decided to build an airport where the previous gravesites were built. A firefighter's helmet sits on top of a granite log. Graves of bankers and artists and politicians and dogs and soldiers and children. I see a tomb in memoriam of the hundreds of passengers who died on a cruise ship that crashed in a nearby body of water almost two centuries ago.

We keep walking. Black marble slats go on forever in every direction, punctuated by larger tombs of the dead and moneyed, a dedication to all they could not take with them, often adorned with a weeping angel, as if they were crying, "oh, what could have been?"

We keep walking. I want to give up. "We're never going to find him, are we?" I ask.

"Don't give up. Come on. Just think about a joke grandpa would make about myopia or something," Sophia says.

"I don't think I knew him when I was old enough to understand his jokes."

"Fair point."

"What a shame, to be cut off from a generation so close. I mean, I know people who even got to know their great-grandparents. Jesus, the things you could ask that generation."

"Well, maybe you should settle down and have kids and you'll have someone to ask you those questions," Sophia suggests unsolicited.

I shoot her a look. "Don't start."

"Right, right, because what's the point of procreation in a world that's already in ashes. That's what you usually fall back on isn't it?"

I grab the bottle of wine from her and unscrew the top. "Yeah, something like that. I have my poetic side." I take a drink. "Remember, when we were growing up, I was fascinated by natural disasters?"

"Vaguely," Sophia says.

"I miss that most about Mom. She might hate me now, but I loved when she took me to the library. You remember how the kid's section was in the basement? And there was a window into a courtyard that no one could actually enter. But there was a tree that grew there. I remember that tree more dead than alive. I don't think it could possibly have gotten much sunlight. That building's been torn down for, what, twenty years? More? Why is it that the passage of time makes less sense the older one gets? 'I can't believe it's already been a year,' 'I can't believe it's already been a decade,' we say. As if we haven't been experiencing this passing for our whole lives. What is it we are trying to claim? A person born is never innocent. Think of the word innocent and how it ever applies to a person born especially in this country. Is it possible to be innocent and complicit at the same time? Why are we so concerned about fault and blame?" I pause, stop walking, and take a sip of wine. "But I would sit by that window, in that musty basement, and just devour these books about tornadoes, earthquakes, hurricanes. All of these natural forces that people have tried to shield themselves from since the beginning of time. Eventually, I just realized that humanity wasn't just in an uphill battle against nature. It was a war of attrition that we can never win. It's impossible. And we still continue to build in the most adverse conditions. It's absurd! We're surrounded by fires that we don't know how to control even though we started them. We throw away everything in the ocean and wonder why it's hurling everything it has back at us. I realized over time that this is not just man's relationship to nature, it's man's relationship to himself." I pause to drink. We are standing in the cemetery surrounded by death. A few birds chirp a melancholic funeral march, or at least that is what I imagine them to be singing. The sun is almost entirely down, but an orange glow creeps over the fading horizon. Sophia does not look at me as I ramble. "You see, man is most destructive against himself. We can learn absolutely everything we want to about health and relationships and ethics and something new will just come up that makes us self-destruct. There's no such thing as a complete human, right? Any happiness is only temporary right? So what is eternal? It's destruction. It's destruction of the self, it's destruction of society, and it's destruction of the world." I see a tear start to swell in the corner of one of Sophia's eyes. Her beautiful eyes, the color of leaves in autumn used to look like.

"You sure put a lot of faith in humanity," she chokes out.

"Look, I know it's absurd to be that egotistical about what people can do. But I mean, I don't know, I wish I could see this world after humans have destroyed themselves. Like, give me a time machine, so I can just see this world as it is. Without all the noise and all the people and all the chaos."

"There will still be chaos, C."

"Yeah, but it will be a pure chaos. Not this bastardized, self-aggrandizing, grandiose human-made bullshit chaos."

The tear has made its way down Sophia's cheek and she turns to me. "What is the point of all of this?"

"I don't know."

"You're obsessed with something you lost years ago, but you leave the people around you now in a rubble you don't see. Susan hates you. Mom and Dad hate you. I don't even know why I try to rebuild our relationship sometimes. You're a desert leaving everyone who cares about you dying of thirst because you don't know how to love. Love isn't creation or destruction, and it's not a binary. If you weren't so focused on what you have already decided is inevitable you could see that. Instead you keep cutting yourself off and—"

"You are no one to judge me. You've never been honest with anyone in your life!"

I stop. Sophia takes a deep breath and lets it out. We stand in silence.

"How the hell did we start on all this?" Sophia asks.

"I don't know." I take a sip of wine and hand the bottle to Sophia. "Do you really think I'm incapable of love?"

"I don't know. Not more than anyone else. I just know you better than everyone who hasn't lied to me yet."

"I almost feel like there was a compliment in there somewhere."

"Only someone without a shade of modesty would think that." She pauses. "We never found Grandpa. He would probably make a joke about how in hindsight we should have planned this out better."

"In hindsight, I should have been less of an asshole," I say.

"In hindsight, I never should have given up on you," she says.

The 13th Defenestration Day

Others have been better about rebuilding since the attack. But I am shattered. Most things that shatter can be rebuilt. The pieces are all still there and all you have to do is connect the pieces in a new creative way. It's called problem solving and people have done it for millions of years. I threw away my shattered pieces like that broken jar. There are a million jars in the world, and I decided mine wasn't worth repairing.

Every day was Defenestration Day after Joy died. It was all noise. I hadn't participated in a Defenestration Day since the attack, and I hadn't participated in much else either. I was resigned. I had completely become all the things that I did not have…which is to say, I had nothing.

I left my apartment. I couldn't be there anymore. Her ghost was haunting me. I wandered for weeks. It might have been months. I didn't speak to my sister. I didn't speak to my parents. I had no one. I barely had myself. Six years later I was living downtown where it's less poetic but more intoxicating. I spent every day drunk, the world blacking out around me, the power grids going down. I couldn't communicate with anyone, though I didn't have anything to say anyway. I couldn't be the only one who felt like this, but also it's entirely possible that I was.

With the 13th Defenestration Day approaching, I didn't want to remember all the things I was no longer allowed to say. I read my grandfather's old optometry textbooks in the hopes that I could better understand vision, that I perhaps would be able to pull back the curtain that's hiding what I've been looking for:

REFRACTION

AND

HOW TO REFRACT

meaning

may be defined as energy

waves

velocity

substance

intensity

A Positive **Focus** is the point

after

A Negative **Focus**

Reflection. – From the Latin *reflectere*, "to rebound." This is the sending back of rays of light by the surface on which they fall into the medium through which they came. While most of the rays falling upon the surface of a transparent substance pass through it, with or without change in their direction, yet some of the rays are reflected, and it is by these reflected rays that surfaces are made visible.

The *appearance* of an image in a mirror is not

the same as that of the object facing the mirror

The place where the

secondary ray in-

tersects the image

diminishes the principal focus.

a real inverted image

is always true.

an object is

distant and

inverted

beyond

focus.

Refraction. – From the Latin *refrangere*, meaning "to bend back" – i.e., to deviate from a straight course. Refraction may be defined as the deviation which takes place in the direction of rays of light as they pass from one medium into another of different density.

Two laws govern the

deviated.

The ray continues in its original direction,

but has deviated from its course; it has undergone

displacement.

pass out into a rare medium.

Effect of a Prism. – An object viewed through a prism has the appearance of being displaced.

detect

damages

escape

blindness

create sympathy.

the face

contradicted the mind

the eye receives

a false image.

Infinity

is

distant.

The Room. – This should be darkened by drawing the shades or closing the blinds; the darker the room, the better.

Whenever there is any

disturbance in

equilibrium

spoken of as
imbalance

the two eyes cannot

see without correcting

the point of fixation.

perfect balance

perfect fixation

imperfect equilibrium

a tendency to deviate inward.

It was useless. It was meaningless. Because how can a book about seeing help you find something you don't even know you're looking for? What was I missing in the emptiness? And what could I learn from a man that used cigar wrappers as bookmarks? How could I have ever drifted so far from everything that brought me into this world?

The Night Before the 20th Defenestration Day

I leave Sophia. I tell her that I might need to be alone for the rest of the day. She hesitates but I can tell that she can tell that it's important I spend some time by myself.

I don't walk home. Enough walking for one day. If only I could have lived in a city with reliable public transportation, though I'm not sure those even exist anymore. Instead I have to click around the device in my pocket until I find an auto to pick me up that I can afford.

What was that all about? Natural disasters and optometry and vision? And all of this stuff from when I was growing up…is that still me? I've lived so much, or so I tell myself. I don't feel as though I relate to the same body that had those experiences, despite being connected by the memories. All of the philosophers and psychologists and all of those people that can hold a conversation for more than ten minutes without drinking were right. Identity is fluid. It's not an illusion; I want to believe it's an illusion. But it is there, just not a solid state, it is there in a fluid state, like glass, the illusion is that it is solid. Identity is goddamned sand and all of our experiences are little tiny grains and consciousness is the beach and even all of the little grains we cannot see are still present they still exist they exist below the surface and the lucky few get to take a metal detector across the existence of their consciousness to discover what really lies beneath while the rest of us are content to sunbathe and maybe take a dip in the sea occasionally when life gets too hot for us to stand.

Wow, Sophia was right to cut me off. I want to go to a bar, but I should not go to a bar. There was a time in my life when I voraciously read memoirs by recovering alcoholics. Some of them were better than others, but they all made me want to drink more. My drinking memoirs wouldn't be exciting. No one needs to read about vomiting in a cab, about being at my best friend's thirtieth birthday party and complaining about being unemployed and a failed writer and making the evening all about me; about drunken romantic encounters that had nothing to do with romance; about all the same sorry clichés that everyone who has ever relinquished the ability to say no, to give in to impulses, be they drink or sex or power or language or death or a combination or absence thereof.

The auto I have tapped to pick me up arrives. I get in, and there is or isn't a human driver. Hard to tell. I have already put in my home address. We glide through city streets, windows up between me and the city, the city that is simultaneously on fire and underwater, a roar of cacophony that drowns out anything intelligible, making the city demur in a way that contradicts the height of the buildings, the strength of its bridges, the lush beauty of its gardens, the calls of the myriad birds and prey and birds of prey that pry through the air like the calls of lost souls that will spend all day tomorrow defenestrating. For what. For what for what for what. To throw away words? Isn't there enough of that? Haven't we already figured out that the ways which we communicate are not actually communication? All of these words that we use over and over and over again.

The car stops. Language is all over. Everywhere and nowhere.

Now, here at my apartment, the four stories it takes for me to reach my front door and unlock it with a key that I have in my pocket just seems too daunting. Because the sooner I go up there, the sooner it will be tomorrow and I will hear all of the calls, the ceaseless voices, all blending into one, all saying the same thing, perhaps with different words, but all trying to connect. The louder we call out, the harder we are trying to connect. Yet no one responds. And if they do, we lose the language to be able to call back.

I can't go up those stairs. Those stairs to tomorrow. I lean my back against the concrete wall. I stare at the moon. Banks and men with billions in banks will soon colonize that large rock just for the chance to create a new language and destroy it the way we are destroying our language now. Did we ever even have a culture worth protecting? At this point, everything that has happened seems inevitable. The way we use technology, the way we use language, the ways we fight, the ways we hurt, the ways we hurt ourselves and hurt others, the ways in which we anger, the ways in which we scar our bodies to feel something, because we fail to see past our own skin, to see that we are all the same, we all want the same things, we all want the powers that clichés give us, we are fortunate to live in a time to have been exposed to the wisdom of billions of people that have survived before us. And what do we go on and do with it?

Destroy it.

With this thought in mind, with the inability to walk up the stairs, I walk around the corner. A couple neon lights. A tile mosaic in front of a wooden door that requires a bit of a shove. The sounds of piano, of upright bass, of drums gently brushed greet me, an old man sitting on a stool at the bar turns his head.

"Well there's a face I ain't seen in a quite some while," he says.

"Don't get used to it," I sigh. "It's been a long day. Tomorrow's going to be a longer day."

"Tomorrow's gonna be a longer day," he repeats. "They're always getting longer til they ain't. Take advantage of it while you can."

"I didn't come here to talk about that, man. I just came here for..." I trail off not knowing how that sentence is supposed to be finished.

"You know exactly what you came here for but you don't want to say it. You don't have the words for it, as you usually like to put it. You exist in a language-based society, you write for a living, and here you are, so conveniently out of words."

"Convenient is not the word I would use, but yes, here I am. Here we are." I motion to the bartender and he walks over, polishing a glass. "That looks clean enough. Mind dirtying it with whatever your cheapest pint is?"

Without a word, he takes the glass, fills it up with water disguised as a lager, and places it in front of me. He says it's three dollars, and I give him four. I take a sip. I take another sip.

"You're thirsty," the old man says.

"I'm always thirsty these days. That's my problem. Nothing satisfies me anymore." As the words are coming out of my mouth, I am thinking how little I want to get into this conversation but it's already happening so I continue. "That's not totally true. I can't be satisfied with the things I have, but I never come across anything new that seems worth my while. What the hell do I do?"

"Stop running from your past for one," he replies bluntly.

"Christ, you make it seem so easy. Cool, guess I just start doing that now." I take a gulp of the lager.

"Why do you think tomorrow is so important for you?"

"It's important for everyone."

"That's not true, and that's also not a reason."

"She's dead, Sam."

"I'm not talking about her," the old man says. "Don't you get it by now? This is all about you."

Sam looks away from me to the bartender, content to check his mobile. No back up for Sam today. "Let's think about it another way," he says and takes a sip of the brown liquid in the short glass in front of him. "Imagine your life. Imagine your life without language. Who would you be instead? Would you still be you? Would you still be you if you couldn't speak? What if you had thoughts that you could not speak? Are you still you then? Think about all of the thoughts you have on a daily basis that you don't tell your family, that you don't tell Sophia, that you don't tell lovers, that you don't tell Susan."

At this I finish my beer. "Sam, you know I don't have anything to do with Susan anymore. I told you that was over a long time ago."

"Yeah, that's what you told me, but give me some credit here. Besides, like I said, language has more power over you than you realize. It makes you not you. Blessing and a curse, as they say."

I hate Sam's ramblings, but part of me also knows he's right. How the hell does he know that about Susan? I haven't even told Sophia about anything like that. "So what's your point with all of this? That I'm not actually who I am? What's the point, Sam?"

Sam takes a sip of his drink. "The point is this. Don't trick yourself into actually thinking you get to choose what happens. It's not for you to choose. You are only a vehicle. A sad-ass vehicle with an empty beer at a bar he hates, talking to an old man that he couldn't care less about."

"Come on, Sam, you know that isn't true."

"I know it isn't, C. But do you?"

I crack my head to the left without responding verbally. I wave to the bartender and point to my empty glass. He begins to fill up a new one and places it in front of me. I participate in my half of the waltz, and place another four dollars on the bar.

The 17th Defenestration Day

All of them riddles. Some meant to be decoded. Some not.

All of it I can hear and I cannot see.

It's the yesterday

What a record for tonight for how cool we are

Just wait til you know you're joking

We are already corpses

It's all warehouse parties, decrepit

Honestly...I would too

If he's probable got the waterfall with anxiety?

I've got the U.S. — including the history of Love

4 of 5 stars to Sex

Cyclists tired of the word storytelling

Me: Politics!

Wow. No. Never. And the headlines today!

Honestly...I would too

I can't afford NOT to make this. Will there be...

Which direction to the Department of Questions

Cole writes an illusion

Not able to hear this but only time no talk.

From the experiences before/during/ after being

Feeling Chilly? Bones Ache? Still ill?

No more endless scrolling

Me acknowledging the station where drivers yell inaudibly

I can't afford NOT to walk with anxiety turned on

Love! Love!

Wait til you don't think I'm playing

All of them riddles. Some meant to be decoded. Some not.

All of it I can hear and I cannot see.

I consider myself fortunate enough to…

Feeling Chilly? Bones Ache? No Ambition?

Most drivers yell inaudibly at a writing job blues

Three of the trash, four of the year, five of

the Earth

I can't afford NOT to slowly join the Department of the Lonely

How do I forgive him to convince me?

I threw myself down the stairs

Anything could be true, depending on the context

Candles burn behind the façade of my face

Hands on a mirror and nothing is clearer

That's when I reached for my revolver

Don't look back and don't look forward

The birds are flying away, depending on your perspective

It's not a gasp, it's a prayer

A western swoop perches over a square

Grass too can grow out of woods

An open window still lets light into the darkest room

The wheels still spin in the snow

It's gone and it won't come back…it will come back

Every cloud is transparent

Green explodes into red with the right tint

Said the lion to the lamb

To cross and un-to-cross

A question is a question in a box

Nothing is sharper than a definition

Red curtains will always be on fire

All of them riddles. Some meant to be decoded. Some not. All of it I can hear and I cannot see.

A triangle is always made of four lines

You can't always see the fourth line

There are no other dimensions

You're just not looking close enough

The circle is never complete

It looks complete

And again

Maybe you're just looking too close

And still fail to see the gaps in the lines

I understand

A spiral can be confusing

And not because it just won't be straight with you

Let me be straight with you:

Whenever you think you have left the bubble

You are still a tree

Forming in the cracks of granite

Your shadows

Are from candles

You are still a waterfall

You are still decrepit

You are endless

You are caught in the wheels of time

And you

Are still

In the bubble

All of them riddles. Some meant to be decoded. Some not. All of it I can hear and I cannot see.

The 20th Defenestration Day

Around midnight, I leave Sam and the bar, and I return to my apartment. I walk to my windowsill and pick up a flat stone that I found on a beach one time. I rub it firmly, attempting to turn it into dust, but all I am doing is rubbing the dirt off my own fingers. I stick the rock in my mouth and begin to suck on it, for no other reason than the tactile experience. Perhaps the only true feeling I have had all day. No. That's not true. That is unfair to Sam, to Sophia, to Susan.

I think about my dedication to this holiday. To this damned holiday. To the significance it holds and if that significance is any more real and true than any other day of the year. Even after I stopped celebrating it still held a grasp over me. To be ruled by a holiday, to be ruled by time. Is that worse than to be ruled by another human? A lover? To be ruled by a nation? It is all ruled by language. Try as I might to condemn it, to condemn defenestrating, to condemn language, to condemn love and life and the pursuit of happiness, I come up short. I fail in condemnation.

I stand in my room wondering what the morning will bring. It is not yet light out, but daybreak is not far off. My thoughts inevitably return to the first Defenestration Day. I think about how I used to have so much. I used to have so much to say. But even then, I mostly focused on what it was I did not have. I focused on what was not there in my life. I used to think that knowing the absences that are present in one's life is a way to name the void and therein laying the foundation of being able to fill it.

Was that wrong?

The artist's most valuable asset is a blank canvas. The musician's most valuable asset is silence. The writer's most valuable asset is the blank page.

What is it that I am missing that is the most valuable part of my life?

I used to throw my words out the window. Like everyone else. The words that I would no longer need. Because I used to know what I needed. Or I thought I knew what I needed. And now that there is an even larger void to fill, I no longer know how to fill out.

I think about that last time I saw Joy. I think about how all of that which we did not say was more powerful than all of the memories we threw away that day. How all of the really meaningful aspects of our relationship could never be written down or said. I see how I pushed her away, about this silly game that she put up with every year that I did not appreciate enough in the moment. She sacrificed her time for me. She could have been working toward something else. She could have gotten out of this decrepit city. Instead we built our relationship and cherished it like a monument. And after that foundation is gone, how do we stand when Earth feels more like a foaming sea than solid land? The people we love most in life, the things we love most in life, can be ripped away and ripped apart in seconds, their physical being dissolved, and yet their ghosts will haunt every corner of a city. A boulevard is just as likely of a setting as the top of a hill to be haunted by everything that you've ever let pass you up in life. Maybe that's why we make promises to never let it happen again, and then constantly let it happen again.

I walk to the window and open it. The night is still, in the way that the air can be still between yourself and another person right before they announce to you they have cancer, the way stillness is present right before the wheels of an airplane hit the runway asphalt, the way stillness persists in a world that is always changing. The stubborn drums of history get louder and louder the faster we careen toward the future. And yet tonight, itself stubborn against the coming day, remains silent and still, resistant against the inevitable, lighting a candle of hope that perhaps the concept of inevitability was not created from the dust of the universe, but a man-made concept, and thus fallible, thus not inevitable, after all.

No one is walking on the streets at this hour. There used to be so much energy in this city, a vibrant urban paradise with life embedded in every crack on the sidewalk. I am sure it still exists somewhere but it gets harder and harder to find. Am I just not looking hard enough? Of course it can be a combination of both. So many questions I have asked left unanswered. Then again, answers are never as satisfying as we want them to be.

Why do we miss so much the things that we miss? Why are we so selfish? I want to take back every word I have ever thrown out a window. I want to take back every fist I've ever swung. But then, what would I have?

I still wouldn't have Joy.

Joy knew about Susan and I know how I feel about Susan, how I really feel about her and won't admit to myself. Because of fear? Of change? Because after I lost Joy, I never knew what it was I wanted anymore? What use did I have of language or connections when all it brought was a downward spiral, romantically, professionally, and socially, that has culminated in nothing but a dictionary of words that I used to know? I realize that I never grew up. Taunting Susan the way I did. It's not cruel to be kind, it's just cruel to be cruel. And then I act as if I deserve more. I suppose it's not easy to realize one's own faults that they detest in others but I have to admit that I am not above being jealous. I don't even want to have kids, but to think about her and Flynn—it stirred something in me.

What do I still have of Joy? Again, I return to everything I do not have. I don't have her cooking. I don't have her damp forehead and sour breath waking up next to me under the sheets every morning. I don't have any diseases she could have given to me like in a tragic novel I read once. I can't hear the vibrations of the strings on the guitar she used to play for me—they have all evaporated into the celestial ether. But I do have a wallet she gave me. I have plastic peacock feather decorations. I have handwritten love letters. I have problems with alcohol I've never been able to shake.

I think of the cave that my life has become. Nothing in here feels real. Everything I have is a shadow flickering a mirage of everything that used to be there. My life is a grotto filled with shallow water reflecting a distant moon. I dig a trench but bullets keep flying closer to my head. Even if there were a light straight at the end of the tunnel, I still wouldn't be able to find my way to it.

I want to scream this all out the window but I know it is still too early. Then again, is there any penalty? Is there a fine? Will I be arrested? I've never heard of that happening to anybody. Do I dare try it…?

"MY LIFE IS A SHADOW FROM A CANDLE FLICKERING ITS FORMER SELF!" I scream out the window.

I wait for a response.

I wait for sirens.

Nothing.

Not every venture yields a gain.

I think I may prefer the shackles of my crime just to prove that it meant something. But now my only shackles are that which imprison me to perpetually live in the past. With no foresight. And barely hindsight at that.

Where did all the music go?

Why did I act like that with Susan?

By now I should know better than that. Of course, when you've been dishonest with yourself for so long, you forget what it looks like to have an identity. If I hadn't been throwing away my words all these years, I could still use them wisely.

And of course, Sophia. If I ever have a final memory before the last breath escapes my lips, I want to think of Sophia. I don't tell her enough what she means to me in my life because I have some stupid idea that as siblings we already know this about each other. Even when we seem like completely opposite people. Even when it seems like we actually come from different families. Even when I disagree with her or think she's being annoying. She is my sister and a point of luminescence in this too often staid world.

Will she think of me when she dies?

Will Susan?

When was the last time Joy thought of me? Right before her death? A day before? A week? Months? We have no way of knowing how much we still linger in the minds of those who used to love us. And how present we have to remain to be aware of all the universal love in this world.

We don't hold on. We hate holding on but holding on is all we have.

Holding on is all I have.

And I continue to let go and go and let go and go and let go and go and let go and go and let go...

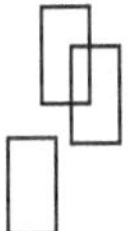

I dozed off at some point. Lost in my revelry for a time I will never get back, nostalgia for that which I never lived. Clouds blot out the sky and a light drizzle begins to fall. The sun attempts to shine through but only provides the lowest amount of ambient light. Nonetheless, day is broken, and words begin to explode like fireworks. Words like bangs and pops and cackles and whistles. Language like sirens. A barrage of alarms.

The coiled whispers of everything that bleeds

A pink forest springs eternal.

Cones of prime evil dedicate a lifetime to suffering…

Keep your arrow aimed at the star

A diamond followed
by another diamond
is a diamond

Count to ten and shine for me!

All of them riddles. Some meant to be decoded. Some not.

All of it I can hear and I cannot see. Today is the day.

Today is Defenestration Day.

Andrew Hertzberg is a reader and writer living and alive in Chicago. He self-published the short story and poetry collection *The Sins of Reality/What Should I Be Doing With My Hands?* in 2018. His work has been featured in Belt Publishing's Rust Belt Chicago: An Anthology, *Motley* Magazine, *Post-Trash, Moonglasses* Magazine, *Since I Left You, Third Coast Review, Cheat River Review*, and elsewhere. He doesn't have an MFA.

www.andrewhertzberg.com

ACKNOWLEDGEMENTS

The deepest gratitude to everyone at Parafine Press for making this a physical thing: Anne Trubek, Martha Bayne, William Rickman, Meredith Pangrace. To David Wilson for the perfect cover. A special thanks to Dan Crissman, for helping me clarify so much in this work and letting the narrative dive into the ambiguity without drowning.

To Keith Meatto, for helping me grow as a writer and being a committed and thoughtful editor many moons ago. To Leo Lopez, Peter Lillis, Jordan Mainzer, Tim Myers, Kati Heng, and everyone else that worked together on Frontier Psychiatrist, a true community I was proud to be a part of.

To the *Disintegration Loops* and Pantha Du Prince, to Italo Calvino and Albert Markovski, Julius and Joana, Francis Bacon and Jessica Hagedorn.

To Craig Arnold, for being both an early inspiration and champion of my writing and giving feedback on so many stories over the years, most of which have never seen a physical form. To Adam Lawson for giving me the courage to say, "fuck it" and just publish something already. To Kelly Cunningham and *Motley* Magazine for taking a chance and publishing some weirdo poems of mine. To Kerri Hacker, for responding with the word "Defenestration" when I was crowd-sourcing ideas for short stories on [redacted social media platform]. To friends who were totally accepting of me saying "I need to stay in and write a story about screaming out windows tonight." You are all too many to name and yes, if you're reading this, you know who you are and please give me shit next time you see me for not mentioning you on this page. To all my family, my brother, my mom, my dad.

To anyone who picked up this book from the title and thought it would have anything to do with Prague and the Thirty Years War of 1618. To every publication that rejected the flash fiction version of the first chapter – you were right, it needed something more.

www.ingramcontent.com/pod-product-compliance
Lightning Source LLC
Chambersburg PA
CBHW070507170726
48291CB00008B/2692

* 9 7 8 1 9 5 0 8 4 3 0 5 3 *